I Need a Hug!

Written and illustrated by first-grade students of Clara Barton Elementary School in Bordentown, New Jersey: Ashley Andrews, Paul Andrews, Eric Arroyo, Eric Bankhead, Maurice Coleman, Rand Geiger, Amanda Horner, Danny Immordino, Scott Ketterer, Tommy Lynch, Tabitha Moran, Chris Moscatiello, Kevin Porter, Kristen Rutherford, Brett Sheehan, Sara Spink, and Brynn Tunney.

Coordinated by Clara Barton Elementary School teacher Marilyn Hartford.

Willowisp Press®

Published by Willowisp Press
801 94th Avenue North, St. Petersburg, Florida 33702

Printed in the United States of America

6 8 10 9 7 5

ISBN 0-87406-605-0

"I'm alone and sad," said one red bug.
"What I need is a big bug hug!"

Two green bugs dug and dug.
Red Bug said, "I need a hug!"
"We are digging. Go away.
Please come back some other day!"

Three orange bugs with yellow mugs.
Red Bug said, "I need some hugs."
"As you can see, we're drinking tea.
Go away and let us be!"

Four purple bugs with a slug.
Red Bug said, "I need a hug."
"We are busy. Go away.
Please come back another day."

Five black bugs in bed all snug.
"Can I have a hug?" said Red Bug.
"We are still sleeping. Go away.
Will you come back another day?"

Six blue bugs tug and tug.
Red Bug said, "Give me a hug."
"We are tugging. Can't you see?
Go away and let us be!"

Seven gray bugs hold a jug.
Red Bug said, "Give me a hug!"
"This is heavy. We can't stop.
If we do, the jug will drop!"

Eight yellow bugs on a train. Chug Chug.
Red Bug *still* really needs a hug.
"We're on a ride. Go away.
Come back to us another day!"

Nine green bugs on a plug.
Said Red Bug, "I need a hug!"
"We plug this in to play this game.
You can't play. We don't know your name."

Ten pink bugs on a rug.
Red Bug said, "Could I have a hug?"
"We are playing. Go away.
This is *not* the place to stay!"

"I'm still alone and feeling bad.
I need a pal, and friend, a hug.
Without them I'm a sad Red Bug."

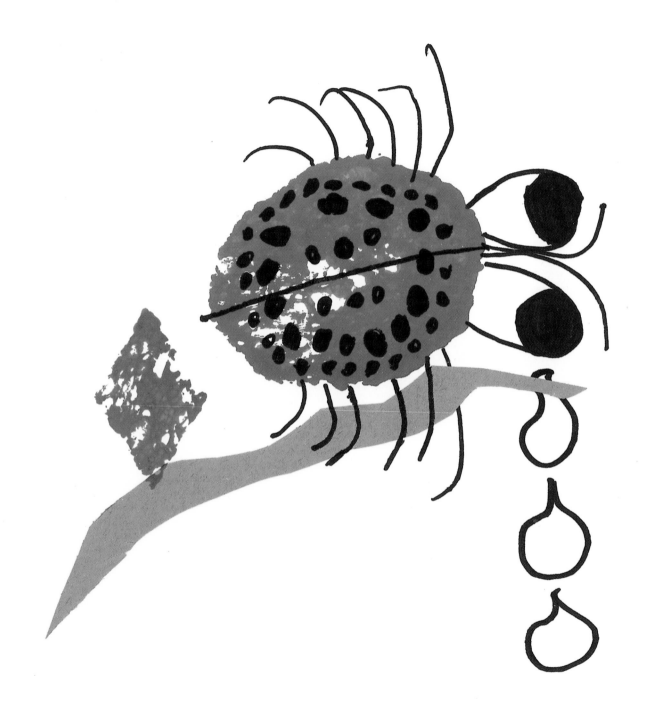

"What is this? What do I see?
Is this a red bug looking at me?"

"I'm alone and I'm sad, too.
What I need is a friend like YOU!"

We're all alike, can't you see?
I'll hug YOU if you'll hug ME!

We all need friends, we all need hugs.
We're all like these two little red bugs!
Before we go we want to say,
"Take time to hug YOUR friend today!"

The Kids Are Authors™ Competition
"Books written by children for children"

School Book Fairs established the Kids Are Authors™ Competition in 1986 to encourage children to read and to become involved in the creative process of writing. Since then, thousands of children have written, designed, and illustrated their own books as participants in the Kids Are Authors™ Competition.

The winning books in the annual competition are published by Willowisp Press and distributed in the United States and Canada.

For more information on the Kids Are Authors™ Competition write to:

In the U.S.A.,

School Book Fairs, Inc.
Kids Are Authors™ Competition
801 94th Avenue North
St. Petersburg, Florida 33702

In Canada,

Great Owl Book Fairs
Kids Are Authors™ Competition
257 Finchdene Square, Unit 7
Scarborough, Ontario M1X 1B9

Winners in the annual Kids Are Authors™ Competition

1993: *A Day in the Desert* (U.S. winner) by first graders of Robert Taylor Elementary School, Henderson, Nevada.

The Shoe Monster (Canadian winner) by first and second graders of North Shuswap Elementary School, Celista, British Columbia.

1992: *How the Sun Was Born* (U.S. winner) by third graders of Drexel Elementary School, Tucson, Arizona.

The Stars' Trip to Earth (Canadian winner) by eighth graders of Ecole Viscount Alexander, Winnipeg, Manitoba.

1991: *My Principal Lives Next Door!* by third graders of Sanibel Elementary School, Sanibel, Florida.

I Need a Hug! (Honor Book) by first graders of Clara Barton Elementary School, Bordentown, New Jersey.

1990: *There's a Cricket in the Library* by fifth graders of McKee Elementary School, Oakdale, Pennsylvania.

1989: *The Farmer's Huge Carrot* by kindergartners of Henry O. Tanner Kindergarten School, West Columbia, Texas.

1988: *Friendship for Three* by fourth graders of Samuel S. Nixon Elementary School, Carnegie, Pennsylvania.

1987: *A Caterpillar's Wish* by first graders of Alexander R. Shepherd School, Washington, D.C.

1986: *Looking for a Rainbow* by kindergartners of Paul Mort Elementary School, Tampa, Florida.